THIS BOOK BELONGS TO
HIS/HER/THEIR
ROYAL HIGHNESS

◆◆◆◆◆◆◆◆◆◆◆◆◆◆◆◆◆◆◆◆◆◆◆◆◆◆◆◆◆

Whilst the characters and some events in this book are based on historical fact, the storyline and opinions have been adapted and fictionalised for the entertainment of the reader.

Published by Kindle Direct Publishing

Copyright © 2022 by Charlotte Eaton

Illustrated by Victoria Packer

First paperback edition February 2022

ISBN: 9798513476658

Instagram @charlotteeaton_
Facebook Charlotte Eaton
Twitter @charlotteeaton_
TikTok @charlotteeaton_
YouTube Charlotte Eaton TV

THERE'S A KING IN THE KITCHEN

WRITTEN BY
CHARLOTTE EATON

ILLUSTRATED BY VICTORIA PACKER

Divorced Beheaded Died Divorced Beheaded Died Survived

Died Divorced

Beheaded Divorced Died Behea Survived Beheaded Beheaded Divorced

Divorced Beheaded Survived

Survived Beheaded

Divorced

Died Divorced Survived Died

Beheaded

4

In memory of Grandad/Dad

Thanks to Chloe, Katie, Aidan and all who supported and helped me on this exciting venture.

"Off with your head I say; off with your head!"
Hattie heard this as she woke in her bed.
She'd gone to bed earlier than usual that night,
and this bellowing voice was a terrible fright.
Humphrey the cat also pricked up his ears,
how annoying, he thought,
I could have slept for years.

Hattie crept from her bed to the landing outside,
listening so intently as she took every stride.
She could hear strange voices
from the kitchen below,
and they were voices of people she didn't know.

"Off with your head"
the voice bellowed once more,
Hattie thought by now his throat would be sore.
She then crept down quietly
to see who was there,
when she looked in the kitchen,
she froze in a stare.

For sat round the table drinking Mum's wine,
was Henry VIII and his wives so fine.
"You're just in time Hattie" Henry exclaimed,
"Please come meet my wives,
of who I am famed."
Hattie stepped forward
not quite believing her eyes,
this gaggle of Tudors was a total surprise!

"I need your help Hattie,
about what I should do?
My wives are very naughty
(between me and you)."
"I need to decide whether to let them all live,
to let bygones be bygones
and learn to forgive?"

In a rather quivering voice Hattie spoke out,
"What on earth have they done to
make you cross and shout?
The King then began to present all the women,
and tried to explain all their treacherous sinning.

"My first dear wife is Catherine of Aragon,
bore no sons and has an essence of tarragon.
She gave me a daughter as cute as a fairy,
and she will one day be The Queen Bloody Mary".

Catherine stood up to Hattie's surprise,
with a pretty round face and big blue eyes.

"I was married to the king for 24 years
and now this great brute has brought me to tears.
He wanted a son as heir to the throne,
but I couldn't do that so now I'm alone.
He's found another to love so I'll have to leave,
he desires Anne Boleyn,
who wears the green sleeves."

Boleyn interrupted, "I'm his new number one!
but I too failed to give him a son.
I had Elizabeth but he wasn't that keen,
and she was soon to become the
Great Virgin Queen."

Hattie was quite thoughtful
and gave Henry a glare.
"Does it really matter if a girl is your heir?
You just need to grow up Sir
and become more cool,
At the moment your Highness;
you're being a fool!"

"Then he accused me of witchcraft!"
cried Anne; betrayed,
"Had my poor head cut off with the
edge of a blade."

The queens looked at Hattie with anxious frowns,
the king appeared awkward,
adjusting his crown.
Hattie took a deep breath
not sure what she should say,
"Henry I'm shocked,
how could you act in this way?"

At this point Jane Seymour rose from her chair,
"What a marvellous girl, so brave with such flair.
Tell that big man that he just needs to chill,
for his ideas sometimes are not that brill!"

"Aren't you called Jane?" Hattie said with a grin,
"Did you love Henry although he did sin?"
"Yes" said the lady "Jane Seymour's the name,
I bore him Edward to follow his reign.

But I sadly died a few days after,
the palace no longer filled with joy and laughter.
This left Henry looking for another new queen
and my Edward cruelly died at only fifteen."

"Enough of this ladies!" bellowed the King,
"There's Anne of Cleves here,
what tale does she bring?
She is my fourth wife
and she has something to say,
come on my dear fraulein, take it away."

"From Dusseldorf I came and here I stand,
he saw my portrait and asked for my hand.
It wasn't long after he demanded divorce.
The king spread a rumour
that I looked like a horse!"

The queens were all shocked
and frowned in disgust,
the king, embarrassed, about to combust.
He trembled and stuttered,
he was trying to speak,
this behaviour from him was completely unique.

"I'm so sorry dear Anne, I was terribly cruel,
can you forgive me dear? I'm a silly old mule."
Anne smiled quite sweetly
and gulped down her wine,
"That apology was wunderbar, most sublime."

The queens all looked glad as Henry cowered,
then to the floor came Catherine Howard.
"Excuse me" she exclaimed looking down at hubby,
who sat there forlorn and actually quite chubby.

"He beheaded me too,
which I thought was quite mean,
I was the life and soul, such a fabulous Queen!

The king had a tantrum about things in my past,
said the marriage was over and we weren't to last.
I cried and I screamed I was so distraught,
my ghost still haunts the halls of Hampton Court."

"He didn't chop my head off"
then announced Miss Parr,
we hadn't yet heard from this queen so far.
"I was there at the end, by his side till his death,
right by my dear husband
when he drew his last breath.

But I'm known for more than
just the one who survived,
I was bright and ambitious with plenty of drive.
I looked after the country when he was away,
and published my own words,
which was rare in those days.

"That's brilliant" said Hattie
"You followed your dreams.
Sadly, these others lived by stricter regimes.
What have you to say King Henry,
you seem upset?
Are you beginning to feel some pangs of regret?"

The king looked forlorn
as he addressed his dear wives,
"I'm incredibly sorry I ruined your lives.
If I had my time again here on this earth,
I would have made sure that I valued your worth.
You're all beautiful women,
strong, splendid, and true,
but Hattie, now it's time that we talk about you."

Hattie was nervous waiting for Henry to speak,
would his words be uplifting or dreadfully bleak?
"Do me a favour Hattie and go forth and teach,
see how many people you are able to reach.
Tell the children of this world
just how they should be,
that we are all equal;
Yes, you've just made me see!"

Hattie stood addressing the royal flock,
"I'm so glad you've seen sense,
but it's now 12 o'clock.
It's terribly late
and so I hope you don't mind,
I'm going upstairs now as I need to unwind.
I can't wait to tell my friends
about what went down,
Tudors in my kitchen all wearing fancy gowns."

"One more thing though,
we could now change that rhyme.
Things would be different if we went back in time!
You'd no longer be divorced, beheaded or died,
you could just say you partied
and totally thrived!"

Hattie turned from her guests
slowly walking away,
in her heart she just knew
there was no more to say.
She was rather tired as she went up to bed,
Just checking in the mirror,
that she still had her head!

WHAT DID YOU LEARN

ARAGON

_____

_____

_____

BOLEYN

_____

_____

_____

SEYMOUR

_____

_____

_____

ABOUT THE QUEENS?

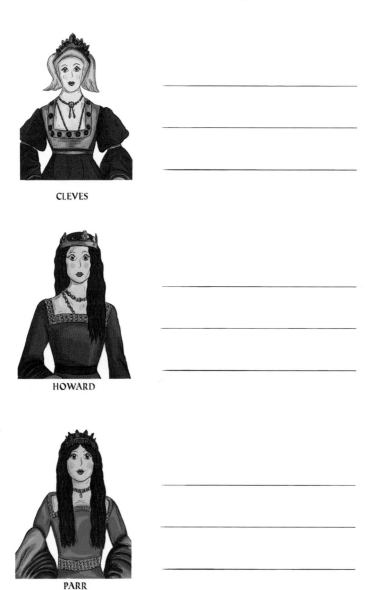

CLEVES

HOWARD

PARR

Died
Survived
Divorced
Beheaded
Divorced
Divorced
Beheaded
Divorced
Survived
Beheaded
Divorced
Beheaded
Died
Beheaded
Divorced

WHAT ARE YOUR OPINIONS OF KING HENRY VIII?

_____

_____

_____

_____

_____

_____

                                                 _____

                                                 _____

                                                 _____

                                                 _____

                                                 _____

                                                 _____

                                                 _____

                                                 _____

Imagine you are a character from the book.

Write a diary entry about your day.

Dear Diary ...

_____

_____

_____

_____

_____

_____

_____

_____

_____

_____

_____

_____

_____

_____

_____

_____

_____

_____

_____

As the king's advisor, what tips would you give Henry about how to be a kinder king?

Henry VIII's

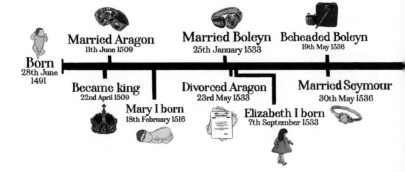

Born
28th June
1491

Married Aragon
11th June 1509

Became king
22nd April 1509

Mary I born
18th February 1516

Married Boleyn
25th January 1533

Divorced Aragon
23rd May 1533

Elizabeth I born
7th September 1533

Beheaded Boleyn
19th May 1536

Married Seymour
30th May 1536

timeline

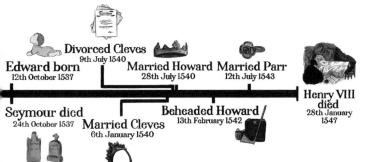

Edward born
12th October 1537

Divorced Cleves
9th July 1540

Married Howard
28th July 1540

Married Parr
12th July 1543

Henry VIII died
28th January 1547

Seymour died
24th October 1537

Married Cleves
6th January 1540

Beheaded Howard
13th February 1542

The End

For my awesome queen
Hattie

Printed in Great Britain
by Amazon